TERROR ON A
TREASURE HUNT

TERROR ON A
TREASURE HUNT

AN UNOFFICIAL MINETRAPPED
ADVENTURE, #3

Winter Morgan

Sky Pony Press
New York

Copyright © 2016 by Hollan Publishing, Inc.

Minecraft® is a registered trademark of Notch Development AB.

The Minecraft game is copyright © Mojang AB.

Sky Pony Press books may be purchased in bulk at special discounts for sales promotion, corporate gifts, fund-raising, or educational purposes. Special editions can also be created to specifications. For details, contact the Special Sales Department, Sky Pony Press, 307 West 36th Street, 11th Floor, New York, NY 10018 or info@skyhorsepublishing.com.

Sky Pony® is a registered trademark of Skyhorse Publishing, Inc.®, a Delaware corporation.

Minecraft® is a registered trademark of Notch Development AB.
The Minecraft game is copyright © Mojang AB.

Visit our website at www.skyponypress.com.

10 9 8 7 6 5 4 3 2 1

Library of Congress Cataloging-in-Publication Data is available on file.

Cover design by Brian Peterson
Cover photo by Megan Miller

Print ISBN: 978-1-5107-0599-9
Ebook ISBN: 978-1-5107-0609-5

Printed in Canada

TABLE OF CONTENTS

TERROR ON A TREASURE HUNT

1
PLANNING

"**W**e've been talking about going on a treasure hunt for such a long time. When are we going?" Lily asked her friends.

Robin agreed, adding, "We want to be prepared. We have to collect supplies. All of those battles with Mr. Anarchy have left our inventories depleted."

Michael looked through his inventory, rattling off a list of items. "Pickaxe, potions, wood, snowballs, apples." He paused. "I think I'm ready for an adventure."

"Great!" Lily exclaimed.

"Is your inventory full?" Simon asked Lily.

Lily checked, then nodded.

Warren walked over to the group. "I found the perfect place to look for treasure."

"Where?" Michael asked.

Warren showed a map to his friends. "There is a large cave in the forest. I heard there is a dungeon there that's filled with treasure."

"Who told you about the dungeon?" Lily asked.

"I met a person in town who was talking about it."

"Who?" Lily was curious to.

"His name is Peter," replied Warren. "He visited the forest and discovered the dungeon. A creeper destroyed him before he could loot the dungeon. And now he wants to go on our treasure hunt."

"When can we meet him?" asked Lily.

"Now," Warren explained. "Peter lives in the village."

The gang followed Warren into town. On the way to the village, they ran into Ilana the Alchemist. She was carrying her chest filled with potions.

"Are you interested in trading? I just brewed some new potions." Ilana opened the large chest.

Lily eyed the potions. "Maybe we should get a few. We are about to go on a treasure hunt."

"That sounds like fun! Can I join you?" Ilana asked the gang.

"Yes," Warren replied. "Of course you can join us. We're going to the forest biome. We have to find my friend Peter, and then we will start to plan the trip."

Simon looked at the sky. "It's getting dark. I think we shouldn't leave until tomorrow."

"But we have enough time for a quick meeting before the sun sets. We can wake up early and start our trip to the forest," Warren announced to the group.

Ilana and the others walked down the town's main street, and Warren pointed out Peter's house. "It's right past the shops," said Warren.

Peter lived in a small house made of cobblestone. He had a patch of land where he grew potatoes and carrots. Outside his house, an ocelot was resting. As they approached the house, the ocelot meowed.

"Peter," Warren said, knocking on the door.

"I'm over here," Peter called to his friends, walking out of his neighbor's house.

Warren introduced Peter to his friends.

"How long have you lived in Lisimi Village?" Lily asked Peter. "I've never seen you around."

"I've been trapped on this server for a while," he replied.

Warren said, "He was also zapped onto the server by Mr. Anarchy."

Peter smiled. "I'm so happy that you guys will be joining me on a treasure hunt. I usually go on my treasure hunts alone, and it isn't that much fun. I'd rather go with friends."

"This is going to be a great trip." Warren nodded in agreement.

Peter said, "After getting destroyed by a creeper on my last treasure hunt, I am going to be a lot more careful on this trip."

The group studied the map and planned their route. "I think we should head to the desert biome to see if we find any desert temples," suggested Robin.

As they talked, the sky was growing darker. Peter placed a torch on the wall of his home to ward off any hostile mobs.

"We have to get going," Lily excused herself and her friends. "We don't want to stay out at night. It's much too dangerous."

Everyone agreed, and Lily and her friends had started to head home when Robin gasped.

A horde of skeletons approached, shooting arrows at the group. Their bones clanged as they marched toward Peter's house.

Lily retrieved her diamond sword from her inventory and fearlessly lunged at the group of bony beasts. Robin hesitated for only a moment before joining Lily in battle, adding the sound of her sword striking bone to the clamor of Lily's fight. But Robin cried out as a barrage of arrows struck her, and as her last heart vanished she was destroyed. "Robin!" Lily cried out.

It was getting darker, making it easy for other hostile and more powerful mobs to spawn in the Overworld. Lily shook as she battled the skeletons. She feared more mobs would spawn, and she was losing hearts. A quick glance around showed her that her friends were doing no better.

"Look out!" Peter cried.

Zombies lumbered toward the town, followed by two block-carrying Endermen.

Lily struck a skeleton with her sword, obliterating it. As she leapt at a zombie, an Enderman made eye contact with her. The lanky mob unleashed a deafening shriek and teleported toward Lily. She sprinted toward the water, but she wasn't fast enough. The Enderman attacked her and she lost her final heart. With a cry, Lily was destroyed, and the sight of her friends still fighting mobs vanished.

The next thing Lily knew, she was respawning in her cottage.

"Lily," Robin said, standing when she saw her friend respawn.

"Robin." Lily pulled her covers off and got out of bed. "We have to go help the others! They're still battling the monsters that destroyed us."

Robin handed Lily a potion of strength, but Lily almost spilled it when she heard a loud blast.

Kaboom!

"That doesn't sound like a creeper, right?" Lily asked her friend.

"No, that sounds a lot more serious." Robin looked frightened.

The duo ran out into the night, wondering what destruction they'd find.

2

THE BIG HUNT

"I can't see. Do you have a potion of night vision?" Lily asked Robin.

Robin shook her head, and the friends dashed toward the center of town in darkness. Lily reached for her sword when she spotted a baby zombie riding a chicken. "Robin! It's a chicken jockey!"

"I see it!" Robin grabbed her bow and arrow, aiming at the rare, hostile mob.

"I've never seen a chicken jockey before," Lily confessed as she aimed her bow and arrow at the small zombie. The arrow pierced the zombie's flesh and it lost a heart.

Robin replaced her bow and arrow with a diamond sword. She leapt at the chicken, avoiding Lily's arrow as it flew toward the baby zombie.

Seeing that Robin was having more luck attacking the mob with her sword, Lily darted to Robin's side and ripped into the zombie with a blow from her powerful sword.

"Robin! Lily!" Simon called out from somewhere in the distance. "We need your help!"

Lily couldn't reply. She was too busy battling this undead mob that rode a white chicken.

Robin slammed her sword into the chicken, destroying it. She reached down and picked up the feathers it dropped.

"Watch out," Lily warned Robin. Though the chicken was destroyed, the baby zombie was still lumbering toward them. Lily clobbered the purple-shirted zombie with her diamond sword. As it vanished, destroyed by Lily's powerful attack, the mob dropped an iron ingot.

"We have to help Simon," Robin exclaimed.

Lily agreed, and the duo dashed through the dark night toward their friends. Simon was in the middle of battling a gang of skeletons. Ilana and Peter must have been destroyed already, because they were nowhere to be seen. Too late, Lily tried to warn him about the silent creeper lurking behind him.

Kaboom!

Simon was destroyed, and Lily and Robin were left to battle the skeletons without him.

Robin plunged her sword into a skeleton, then looked up to see Ilana running towards them with a potion in hand, ready to splash it on a zombie.

"Ilana!" Robin called to the acclaimed alchemist.

Ilana weakened the zombie Robin was fighting with her potion, then used her sword to annihilate the undead beast. "I can help. I grabbed more potions when I respawned at home." Ilana splashed potions on the cluster of zombies that surrounded Lily and Robin.

"Thanks!" Lily could barely speak as she struck her sword against the bony mobs.

"I got one," Robin exclaimed when she destroyed a skeleton.

Ilana splashed more potions and Lily and Robin obliterated the remaining skeletons.

"What was it that blew up?" asked Lily. "Besides Simon, I mean."

Ilana frowned. "Simon's house, and Juan's butcher shop."

Lily was devastated. They had spent the past few months rebuilding Lisimi Village, and now someone was destroying it.

"Who is responsible for this?" Robin cried.

Ilana shook her head sadly. "I don't know." She paused, then added, "Mr. Anarchy isn't able to grief anymore, so I assume it's someone we don't know."

This scared Lily. She didn't like the idea of an unknown person in their village, especially someone who would threaten them. The villagers had already paid their dues when they battled Mr. Anarchy, and she didn't want to be involved in any other griefer battles. She simply wanted to go on the treasure hunt.

"The sun is rising," Robin said with a smile. She was glad they'd be safe in the daylight.

As she spoke, the rest of the group came running over to them, having respawned in their homes. Lily was relieved to see that Simon had been able to respawn in Michael's home, where he had spent the night before.

Everyone spoke at once. Michael was talking about the explosion. Warren paced while screaming about monster spawners. Juan was crying about his butcher shop. Peter asked about the treasure hunt.

Lily shouted, "Stop! One at a time."

Warren looked at Lily. "This isn't the work of Mr. Anarchy. We have to get to the bottom of the attack."

"Maybe someone from the town is trying to terrorize us." Lily mused.

Everyone paused, uncomfortable, until Michael broke the silence. "Everyone here is a suspect."

"A suspect?" Lily asked. "Us, too?"

"Until we know who has destroyed Simon's house and Juan's butcher shop, we're going to have to keep a close eye on the entire town," explained Michael.

Lily knew she was innocent, and she trusted her friends. But, come to think of it, she knew nothing about Peter. He seemed to have appeared from out of nowhere, and yet he said he'd been in Lisimi Village a long time. How was that possible?

Robin said, "I don't want to think of everyone in the town as a suspect. It's not a good way to look at things. It's not healthy."

"What's your plan?" Michael questioned Robin.

"I think we should prepare ourselves by keeping an eye on the town, but we also have to see what happens next," Robin told him.

"We have to wait for someone to attack us again?" Michael was appalled. "That's an awful idea."

Michael and Robin debated the many ways they could solve this issue, but they couldn't agree on anything.

Peter interrupted. "I think we should focus on the treasure hunt. We want to loot that dungeon. It'll be a great way for us to replenish our supplies, and it's going to be a lot of fun, which will take our minds off of the trouble in the village—maybe it will even help us get a fresh perspective and see who could have done this." When he saw he had everyone's attention, Peter went on. "It's the start of a new day. We should get going now, because then we'll have an entire day to get to the dungeon."

Simon added, "I agree with Peter. I don't think we should stick around Lisimi Village debating our next steps. I think we should go ahead with the treasure hunt. My house was destroyed, and I'd love as many resources as I can gather to rebuild. I hope to find those on a treasure hunt."

"Is everybody ready to go on the treasure hunt?" asked Lily.

Ilana looked through her inventory. "I'm ready. And if anyone needs potions, I have a bunch that I'm willing to trade."

Warren was conflicted about going. "But who will guard the town?"

"It'll be fine," Juan the Butcher reassured Warren. "I'll make sure the townspeople will keep any eye on everything. I'm going to have them build an iron golem to ward off zombies, and then ask them to help me reconstruct my butcher shop."

The group gathered their belongings, and Peter pulled out his map, getting ready to guide them.

But before they could leave, a familiar voice called out, "Wait!"

3
CHEATS

The friends were shocked to see Mr. Anarchy standing in the middle of town, alone.

Michael called to Mr. Anarchy, "What's going on? Why are you here?"

Lily was annoyed. "Isn't he supposed to be under constant supervision?"

Warren replied, "He is. I have no idea how he got out."

Lily grabbed her bow and arrow, aiming at Mr. Anarchy.

"Lily, don't! Please," Mr. Anarchy pleaded. "I have something to tell you guys."

Lily held the bow and arrow, but didn't shoot. "Okay, tell us or I'm going to destroy you and force you to respawn in Warren's house, where you belong."

"I found a way to get players off the server," Mr. Anarchy announced proudly.

"How? We have an entire team dedicated to finding out ways to get home. How did you come up with one on your own?" Warren questioned Mr. Anarchy.

"Several nights ago, I snuck out of Warren's house while everyone was distracted by talk of the treasure hunt you're leaving on. I wanted to use a cheat to summon a storm. It was late and I didn't see the creeper behind me, so it destroyed me just as the storm started. When I respawned and ran outside, skeletons surrounded me and I had very little energy left. I noticed a player off in the distance. I called for his help, and he said he'd TP to me. But after he vanished, he never reappeared. I'm sure that when he TPed, he left the server."

"How do you know the player wasn't TPing somewhere else? Maybe he didn't tell you the truth?" Lily found Mr. Anarchy's idea preposterous. You couldn't leave the server by TPing in a rainstorm.

"I thought the same thing," explained Mr. Anarchy. "But once the rain stopped, I went to search for the player. I had seen him around the village before—he alwayswore a black jumpsuit. I looked all over for him, but I still haven't found him. It's been days."

"A black jumpsuit . . ." Robin paused, deep in thought. "I think I've seen him."

"Recently?" asked Mr. Anarchy.

"Actually, no," replied Robin. She hadn't seen the man in the black jumpsuit in days.

"Does anybody know who he is?" Peter asked.

Michael replied, "I think so. If it's the player I'm thinking of, Juan the Butcher introduced me to him. His name is Otto. I know he is friends with Matthew."

"We should go find him," Lily suggested.

Peter clutched the map. He was annoyed. "I thought we were going on the treasure hunt."

"We are," Simon reassured him, "but we have to find out if Mr. Anarchy really discovered a way to get us off this server. Do you really want to wait if we can go home now?"

"Besides, we promised him he could come with us on our treasure hunt," Lily said. "I can't believe we almost left without him."

Everyone halfheartedly turned back toward the center of town. They walked to Matthew's cobblestone house, which he'd built on the shore when he came to the village a few weeks before. The small house had a large picture window that overlooked the ocean. Matthew was a big fan of taking undersea adventures; he was always trading resources with Ilana, who provided him with potions of water breathing.

"Matthew," Warren called out as the group approached his house, but there was no reply.

"I bet he's under the sea, searching for an ocean monument," said Ilana. "He just traded a bunch of carrots for a potion of water breathing."

As she spoke, Matthew emerged from the crystal blue water and walked to the shore, dripping.

"Is it time for the treasure hunt already?" Matthew asked.

Lily shook her head. "Have you seen Otto?" she asked.

"No," Matthew replied. "I haven't seen him in a long time, and I've been worried about him. Is he okay?"

Mr. Anarchy replied, "I think I was able to transport him back to the real world."

"You're trying to help us get back to the real world? But you're the one who trapped us on this awful server." Matthew was shocked.

"Well," Mr. Anarchy confessed, "I only helped him escape by accident. I really wanted him to TP to me."

"That sounds more like you," Matthew said. "Only thinking about yourself."

Mr. Anarchy frowned, but before he could reply, a woman's voice called out, "Can you send me back?" The group turned around and saw a short woman with red hair walking over.

"I can try," Mr. Anarchy said, looking at the woman.

"Great." She was thrilled.

"Who are you?" Lily asked.

"I'm Emma," the woman replied. "I've been trapped on this server for a long time. I live in a small home outside of your village."

Mr. Anarchy nodded. "Well, if you want to give this a try, there's no time like now," he said. Using command blocks, he summoned a storm. The sky grew dark and rain fell on the group.

"You spawned skeletons," Warren cried. The rain was getting harder, the ground was getting wet, and now they had to battle mobs. "This had better be worth it."

Michael leapt at a skeleton. As he struck the beast he yelled at Mr. Anarchy, "Emma, TP! I want Mr. Anarchy to stop the rain."

Emma TPed toward Mr. Anarchy, but after she disappeared, she didn't reappear.

"Stop the rain!" Lily demanded.

Mr. Anarchy used command blocks to end the rainstorm. Everyone waited, holding their breath, as the minutes dragged out.

"So, where's Emma?" Simon asked.

"I think she must be back in the real world," said Mr. Anarchy.

"Could that really be possible?" Peter was dumbfounded.

"I hope so," Lily said excitedly.

"I want to go next," declared Matthew.

Everyone agreed that Matthew could be the next person to TP in the rain. But as Mr. Anarchy started to summon a storm, Lily called out, "Wait! Can you pause for a second?"

Mr. Anarchy looked perplexed. "Okay."

"I want to say goodbye to Matthew." Lily looked at her friend, and tears rolled down her cheeks. "I'm going to miss you. Even though things between us weren't perfect at first, I'm glad we became friends. I hope when you get back to the real world that you will remember us. Please try to find a way to get us off this server."

Matthew nodded seriously. "I will try to get you guys off this server. I promise."

Lily signaled to Mr. Anarchy, and he finished summoning the storm. Skeletons and zombies spawned under the rainy sky.

"TP, now!" Mr. Anarchy called out.

"Okay," said Matthew. He grinned as he started to TP, disappearing.

But just seconds later, Matthew appeared again, right in front of Mr. Anarchy.

Everyone was disappointed, especially Matthew. "What did I do wrong?"

"Nothing," Lily replied. She could see over Mr. Anarchy's shoulder to the shore beyond, where Emma was running toward them.

4
ADVENTURE MAPS

"Emma?" Lily questioned. "You didn't get sent home."

"No, I guess not," Emma said. "I wound up in the desert biome. It was desolate. I looked for other players, but there weren't any, so I TPed back here," she explained.

"I wonder if the man in the black jumpsuit was zapped back to the real world or if he's just living in a new biome, too," Lily mused.

"I don't know." Mr. Anarchy sighed. "I thought if I could help people get off the server, it might make up for some of the bad things I've done. And for the first time in a long time, I had hope." He started to pace, his voice rising. "But what's the point? I can't figure out how to get myself home, or anyone else."

"I knew it wouldn't work," Emma said with a scowl. "We are all trapped here forever."

Lily comforted her. "It's going to be okay. We will get out of here."

Matthew looked defeated, but he agreed with Lily. "That's right. I will work tirelessly day and night to get us off this server."

Emma sighed. "I'm going to head home. I just want to be alone."

"Are you sure you're okay?" asked Lily.

"Fine," Emma replied curtly, and she walked away.

"I don't think I feel up for a treasure hunt after all," Matthew announced to the group. "I need some time with my thoughts. And while you're away, I'll test some new ideas that might help us find our way back home."

"I'll bring you back some treasure," Warren told his friend.

"Thanks." Matthew smiled weakly, still disappointed about the failed escape plan.

Michael walked over to Matthew and, in a hushed voice, he asked, "Since we are leaving on a treasure hunt, is it possible for you to stay with Mr. Anarchy? I don't feel comfortable leaving Lisimi Village without knowing he's being guarded."

"Yes." Matthew nodded. "Mr. Anarchy, are you serious about wanting to redeem yourself? If you promise not to try anything evil, you can work with my team to develop ways to leave the server."

"I'd . . . really like that," Mr. Anarchy said. "Do you mean it?"

"Yes, as long as you stay where I can keep an eye on you," Matthew replied. "And as long as we don't find out that you're behind the most recent griefer attacks. You've been in Lisimi Village for a while and you haven't done any griefing, as far as we know. We have to give you a second chance."

Mr. Anarchy was beaming. Lily looked over and smiled because she knew that she wouldn't have to worry about the sinister griefer while she was on the treasure hunt. She was happy that there was peace in the village, however short-lived it might be.

"Okay, friends," Michael announced. "We should go on the treasure hunt."

Peter was thrilled. "Great. I'll lead the way."

The gang said their goodbyes to Matthew and the others and left Lisimi Village.

Peter studied the map. "We have to go through the cold biome before we reach the dungeon in the forest."

"I want to play in the snow," Simon squealed.

"I don't think we'll have time to play, but we should gather snow to craft snowballs. They are important to have in our inventories," Michael told the group.

As they walked along the shoreline, Peter told the group about his favorite activities in Minecraft. "Before I got zapped onto this server, I loved making adventure maps. I made all these different maps that people would download. It was a lot of fun."

"That sounds cool," said Michael. "I used to love building in Creative mode. I've built skyscrapers and stadiums. And Lily, Simon, and I built a lot of awesome structures together."

Noticing that Lily was teary-eyed, Robin asked, "What's the matter?"

"I don't like talking about what we used to do in Minecraft. It makes me very sad. I know that we'll be fine, but it's just been so long since we've been home. I miss it. I want to focus on what we're doing now." Lily sniffled.

"I feel the same way," Peter confessed. "But I know that one day I'll be back in the real world making adventure maps again."

"I know you're right," Lily replied, "but it's hard to believe we'll ever escape after all we've been through."

The group walked in silence toward the jungle. The path was thick with leaves. "We have to stick together," Peter warned. "We don't want to lose anyone."

Ilana took out shears and made a path for the group. "This will help us."

"How much further is the forest?" asked Michael.

Peter said, "We just have to get through the jungle and the cold biome. It's right outside the cold biome."

"That won't take very long, will it?" Simon was excited to loot the dungeon.

"Yes, it won't be long," Peter reassured them. "We should get there by nightfall, but we might want to move a little faster to be sure."

"I have a potion of swiftness," Ilana announced to the group. "I'm happy to share."

"That sounds like a good idea," Lily said.

"Wait, look over there!" Robin exclaimed. "I think I see a jungle temple".

Warren called out, "I see it, too!"

"We should see if there's treasure," suggested Robin.

Peter scowled. "It could be emptied of treasure. Why are we distracting ourselves with possibilities when we know there is a dungeon filled with loot in the middle of the forest?"

"We aren't in a particular rush," Robin replied.

"Look. We still have another two biomes to travel through." Peter showed the map to the group, pointing to show how far they still had to go.

"But this is a great opportunity," Warren said.

Reluctantly, Peter nodded, joining the others as they dashed to the temple.

Robin led the way into the temple. The mammoth temple was comprised of cobblestone and moss stone, and it stood on the edge of a wide river. She led the group toward the stairs, knowing treasure was most often found on the bottom floor.

"Remember the last time we looted a jungle temple, Simon and Michael?" Lily asked. "We were so excited to get the treasure. It took us forever to figure out how to get the piston door open, but then we found the chest."

Michael smiled and finished Lily's thought. "And it was filled with rotten flesh!"

"And you wanted to eat it!" Simon added. "But Lily stopped you because she thought you'd get food poisoning."

The gang walked down the stairs and toward the puzzle they would have to solve to unearth the treasure.

"This seems a lot more complicated now that we are actually in the game." Lily looked at the piston-trapped door.

"We have to be very careful," Ilana said.

"I told you this was a waste of time," Peter said grumpily.

The gang let out at collective sigh.

Warren stood by the puzzle and began to open the piston door. But just then, the lights went out.

"What happened?" cried Lily.

"Somebody get a torch," barked Warren.

Lily looked through her inventory, but she didn't have a torch. The others didn't either.

"I thought we had full inventories!" Warren said, annoyance creeping into his voice.

"Don't worry, I have a potion of night vision," Ilana told them. "I'll hand it out to everyone. I have enough."

"Great." Lily tried to find Ilana, but it was very dark.

"Where are you, Ilana?" asked Michael.

"Just listen to the sound of my voice," Ilana said, and everyone fumbled in the dark, trying to make their way toward Ilana.

"Help!" Peter cried out suddenly. He sounded desperate and scared.

Without warning, the lights turned back on.

"Peter, are you okay?" asked Warren.

"Somebody stole my map," he replied.

5
A NEW ENEMY

"**W**hat?" Lily was shocked. She looked around the small, dimly lit basement, searching for the map or the person who stole it.

"Can we find our way to the dungeon without the map?" questioned Simon.

"I'm not sure," Peter replied. "We have to find out who took it!"

"It wasn't any of us," replied Simon.

"Are you sure?" asked Peter.

Lily gasped. "Someone also unearthed the treasure!"

Everyone turned to look at the emptied treasure chests.

"They worked fast, and somehow they were able to avoid getting arrows flung at them from the booby traps. All without us hearing them." Michael was in awe.

"There had to be more than one person." Lily paced around the basement.

"They are also very skilled players," Ilana added. "I bet they used a potion of invisibility to escape."

"And a potion of night vision," added Lily.

"Or maybe the people who stole the map and the treasure are right here," Peter said. He narrowed his eyes, looking at everyone suspiciously.

"That's easy to disprove," Warren said. "Everyone, show us what's in your inventories. Whoever has the map or an unusual amount of treasure is the traitor."

The group began to show each other what was in their inventories, but no one had anything that looked suspicious on them. Peter stamped his foot. "Somebody must have hidden the map and the treasure. Tell us who you are!"

"It isn't any of us," Lily said, stepping between Peter and her friends. "I'm sure of it."

"Why?" Peter raised his voice.

"Because I know everyone here very well. I've fought alongside these friends in many battles against Mr. Anarchy. The only new person here is you," Lily said, pointing accusatorily at Peter. "How do we know that you aren't hiding the map? You could have planned this!"

"I think things are getting out of hand," Michael said. "Let's all take a breath and calm down."

"I agree," said Robin. "If we don't work together, we're not going to get anywhere. It's possible that none of us are responsible for this attack. I really do think someone is griefing us. And this time, it isn't Mr. Anarchy."

Michael shuddered. "I think Robin is right. We have a new enemy."

While the friends argued, a creeper silently lurked down the hall. Nobody noticed the silent, explosive mob until it was too late.

Kaboom!

It exploded right next to Peter. With a look of shock frozen on his face, Peter was destroyed.

"Peter!" Warren called out.

"What do we do?" Simon said. "He knows the way to the next temple."

"Let's stay where we are. Hopefully when Peter respawns, he'll TP to us," Michael told the group.

"But I don't want to wait down here in this basement. It seems like someone is targeting us here," Lily said, turning to walk up the stairs.

As they made their way toward the exit, Peter appeared in front of them.

"Guys," Peter said. His face was flushed, and he looked relieved to have found them. "I have bad news from the village. Matthew told me that Mr. Anarchy is missing."

"Missing?" Michael couldn't believe it.

"It's true," Peter said. "The entire town is searching for him."

"What do we do? Keep hunting, or go back to help the town find him?" Lily asked.

"The entire town is looking for him," Robin said. "We can afford to stay on the treasure hunt."

"But we don't have a map," said Michael.

"Or torches," added Warren.

"What if we help everyone find Mr. Anarchy, and then we TP back here to continue our treasure hunt?" Simon proposed.

"Ouch!" Lily cried out, bringing the debate to a sudden end. "I've been hit by an arrow!"

"What direction did it come from?" Ilana looked for the player who had shot the arrow.

"It's too light out for there to be a skeleton attack," Robin said, walking onto the forest path and trying to see through the dense leaves.

"Ugh!" Lily yelped as another arrow struck her.

The group scattered, searching for the person who shot the arrow.

"I've been hit, too," Ilana wailed.

"The arrows are coming from that direction," Michael cried, pointing. He loped toward a cluster of jungle wood trees.

The gang ran behind him, but when they reached the trees Michael had disappeared behind, they didn't see him.

"Michael?" Ilana called out. She inspected the area around the large trees, but he was nowhere in sight.

6

INVASION IN THE OVERWORLD

"Michael?" Lily hollered.

"He's missing." Simon started to shake. "Who would capture our friend?"

"This has to be the work of Mr. Anarchy," Warren said. "We shouldn't have left him in the village. He was probably plotting this the entire time."

Ilana didn't participate in the discussion. She spent her time closely inspecting the area where Michael disappeared, searching for clues. The patch of grass by the jungle wood trees seemed charred. "Do you think we missed hearing an explosion?" she asked the group. "It looks like the grass is burnt. Maybe he was destroyed by a creeper?"

The others walked over to look at the burnt grass.

Lily said, "But what about whoever was shooting arrows at me? They have to be responsible for Michael's disappearance."

"That's true," Ilana replied. "Maybe it was Mr. Anarchy."

"If it's him, he has to be working with a group," Warren said. "He never could do much without his army."

Just then, an arrow pierced Peter's arm, and he cried out.

Ilana ran in the direction the arrow had come from and was shocked to see Emma hiding behind a tree, holding a bow and arrow.

"What are you doing?" Ilana questioned Emma. But as the others ran over to back Ilana up, the sky grew dark and thunder boomed throughout the jungle.

"It's a storm!" Lily cried.

"No!" Robin shrieked. "It's the Ender Dragon!"

The dragon unleashed a deafening roar as it soared low over the jungle, knocking over a tall tree.

Lily and the others sprinted toward the jungle temple and sheltered themselves from the powerful flying beast and the falling trees.

Simon shot an arrow at the dragon, striking its muscular side. It roared in pain.

Robin grabbed her last remaining snowball and threw it at the dragon, costing it a heart.

The dragon flew toward the jungle temple, slamming its strong, scaly wing against the side of the temple. A large chunk of the building crumbled, and the gang dove out of the way of the debris.

Lily raced toward the dragon and ripped into the side of the flying, hostile mob with her enchanted diamond sword. The dragon lost a heart, but it lunged toward Lily and she fell to the ground.

"Help!" Lily called out as the dragon loomed over her. Emma stood nearby, an unreadable expression on her face. She didn't move to help Lily.

Ilana raced toward Lily's side and splashed a potion on the dragon, which weakened the beast.

Robin plunged her sword into the dragon, and with a shriek, the beast exploded. It dropped wings and an egg, and a portal to the End spawned in the center of the jungle.

While Lily's friends helped her up, Simon looked at Emma, who was scurrying toward the portal. "Stop!" he screamed, and he raced in her direction.

Emma didn't turn around. Instead, she leapt onto the portal to the End and disappeared into the toxic world. Nobody followed her.

"Wow, she willingly traveled to the End on her own." Simon shook his head, watching the portal disappear.

"She's a griefer." Lily was furious.

"I bet she captured Michael," Simon said. "How are we going to get him back? I can't stand the idea that he is trapped somewhere and he needs our help."

Peter suggested, "Maybe we should go back to Lisimi Village and come up with a plan. We don't seem to be getting anywhere on this trip."

They all gasped when a familiar voice said, "I can help."

7
SNOW AND SURPRISES

"**M**r. Anarchy?" Lily asked. "Now what do you want from us?"

"I don't want anything from you," Mr. Anarchy replied. "I want to help you."

"Yeah, right. That's not why you escaped." Simon was suspicious.

"Escaped?" Mr. Anarchy said. "I was kidnapped and taken away from the village. I'm not the one behind all this griefing—I'm a victim of it. And I can prove it."

"How?" Lily demanded.

"Follow me," replied Mr. Anarchy.

"Where?" Lily and the others stood frozen with doubt.

"The cold biome. You'll see that I am not the one who is attacking the Overworld," said Mr. Anarchy.

Lily looked over at the others. "I think we should follow him. What do we have to lose?"

Robin asked, "Mr. Anarchy. Can you tell us what we're going to see when we get to the cold biome?"

"You'll see who is behind the attack. They have an elaborate home base set up in the cold biome."

"How do you know?" asked Simon.

"I was captured from Lisimi Village while I was helping Matthew test ways to escape. The griefers held me there, but I escaped."

"Why should we trust you?" Lily asked.

"I can't prove it unless you'll let me show you," Mr. Anarchy said. "There's only one way to find out."

The group exchanged glances and made a silent decision. Together, they hurried to the cold biome with Mr. Anarchy. As they reached the edge of the jungle, they spotted the icy biome in the distance.

Large, icy spikes protruded from the snowy ground. The enormous spikes looked as if their tops could touch the blocky clouds.

"Oh my!" Lily gasped. "I've never seen anything like that before."

"This isn't a very hospitable biome," Mr. Anarchy warned them. "All of the lakes are frozen and there isn't much wood. The people who survive here are quite powerful because they know how to live with very few resources."

"Who are they," Warren asked, "and why won't you tell us?"

There was no need for a reply. When the group took their first step into the icy biome, they saw Otto. He wore his now-familiar black jumpsuit, and standing behind him was Emma. She aimed her bow and arrow at the group.

"Stand back," Emma hollered.

Otto barked orders at an unknown army. "Forces, attack."

Various players dressed in skins ranging from jeans and sweaters to neon jumpsuits emerged from a hole in a large patch of snow. Otto's army was ready to destroy the gang. The vicious players leapt at them with swords, arrows, and potions.

Lily shielded herself from a woman who swung a diamond sword at her, but the sword connected with her arm. Lily was losing hearts.

"Help!" Lily called out.

Mr. Anarchy raced to her side, diamond sword raised high. In a flurry of motion, he finished her battle and destroyed the woman with the diamond sword.

"Thanks." Lily's energy was incredibly low, and she could barely speak. She looked at Mr. Anarchy in shock.

Mr. Anarchy handed her a potion of healing and she took a gulp. Her energy quickly returned to her, and she joined the battle against the large army.

Two griefers dressed in matching orange outfits shot arrows at Lily and Mr. Anarchy. They dodged the arrows and sprinted toward the griefers with their diamond swords raised. Lily plunged her sword into one of the orange people, annihilating him. Mr. Anarchy slashed and stabbed the other griefer with lightning speed, but the griefer seemed to have an infinite amount of hearts.

No matter how many times Mr. Anarchy struck the orange griefer, she didn't seem to lose one heart.

"What is going on here?" he asked Lily.

Lily grabbed a potion of harming and splashed it on the powerful orange griefer, but it didn't make a difference. She seemed to be undefeatable.

Ilana noticed Lily and Mr. Anarchy struggling with the powerful orange griefer. She ran to Lily and Mr. Anarchy and whispered, "I think we should use the potion of invisibility to escape."

But before they could respond, both Lily and Mr. Anarchy were destroyed.

Lily respawned in her bed at her cottage in Lisimi Village. When she woke, she wished it had all been a nightmare, and that her friends would be outside and there would be peace in the Overworld. However, once she left the cottage, she knew that it wasn't a dream—it was reality. Mr. Anarchy stood outside her door, and that meant that her friends were still battling Otto, Emma, and their army.

Mr. Anarchy seemed fixated on the orange griefer. He didn't even greet Lily before starting to ramble. "I don't understand why she didn't lose hearts. It doesn't make sense."

"That's all the more reason that I have to go back to the icy biome and save my friends. Are you coming with me, or not?"

Before Mr. Anarchy could answer, a voice called out, "Lily!"

Lily was thrilled to see Michael hurrying toward them. "Michael!"

"You recaptured Mr. Anarchy!" Michael said.

"Well, actually," Lily said, "I think Mr. Anarchy is working with us."

"What?" Michael was confused.

Lily explained, "He led us to Otto and Emma. They've created a new griefer army in the cold biome and are staging an attack on the Overworld."

"I know." Michael sighed. "That's where I was trapped. But I thought Mr. Anarchy was working with them."

"I'm not," said Mr. Anarchy. "I don't want to grief anymore. When I thought I helped Otto go back to the real world, I was proud of myself. I realized that I don't want to hurt people. I want to help people get back home instead. I can't keep griefing; it will only distract me from my real ambition, and that is to make my way home."

"I understand," said Michael. "We all want to go home. Lily, it's like you said—that if he had hope, Mr. Anarchy wouldn't grief."

"I just wish we didn't have to battle a new enemy, and we could focus on finding a way to get back to the real world instead." Lily looked over at Mr. Anarchy.

"We will defeat this new enemy together, and I promise to work tirelessly to get us off this server," Mr. Anarchy said. "This isn't the first time I've dealt with Otto and Emma. For a long time after I got sucked into this game, I thought I was the first person ever to be zapped onto the server. I thought it was just a glitch, but it was the scariest thing that ever happened to me. For a long time, the only people I spoke to were Juan, Fred, and Harriet because they were the villagers and they naturally lived on this server. It was very lonely."

"When did other players arrive?" asked Lily.

"It was my fault that other players arrived. At first I thought I had found a way to get off the server by asking people if I could join the servers they were on. They would respond and get zapped in here. That's how the Prismarines formed. They were the first people I trapped, but at least at the beginning, I didn't mean to. And I went on believing I had been the first person trapped here, until I met Emma and Otto."

"What are you saying?" asked Lily.

"I believe Emma and Otto were the first players trapped on the server. In fact, I think they were the ones who trapped me."

"Are you sure?" Lily questioned.

"If what I think is true, it means they might be able to help us find out who trapped them on the server. Maybe we can use that information to help us get back home," suggested Mr. Anarchy.

"We need to TP to the cold biome, rescue our friends, and question Otto and Emma," Lily demanded.

"I can't go back there." Michael shook when he heard them discuss the icy biome. "I was trapped there. Emma and Otto are zapping more people onto the server to create their new army. All of these noobs are being trained to destroy us. It's awful."

"We have to stop them," declared Mr. Anarchy.

But at that moment, an arrow struck Mr. Anarchy. Emma stepped out of the shadow of a house. "Stop who?"

8
TRAPPED

michael rushed toward Emma. "You're the reason we're trapped on this server!"

Emma splashed a potion of weakness on Michael, and he used his last heart to deliver a powerful sword blow to Emma's chest, but she didn't even lose one heart. She grabbed another bottle from her inventory and splashed Michael with potion again, destroying him.

Lily slammed her sword into Emma, at the same time shielding herself from the potion Emma tried to splash on her.

Mr. Anarchy hit Emma with his sword but she doused both Lily and Mr. Anarchy with a potion of harming, and they were instantly weakened. Emma took out her enchanted sword and pierced Lily with it. Mr. Anarchy took advantage of her distraction to splash a potion on Emma, but the potent brew only momentarily weakened her.

As Lily and Mr. Anarchy redoubled for another attack, Otto TPed into the village and rushed to Emma's side. "We have your friends trapped," he announced.

"And don't bother looking in the cold biome." Emma's lips curved, unleashing a sinister smile.

"Where are they?" shouted Lily.

"Still on this server," replied Otto. "But that's all we'll tell you."

"Tell us!" Michael demanded.

"We've given you enough clues," Otto said.

"You guys were planning a treasure hunt, right?" Emma laughed. "Well, now you can go on a serious treasure hunt. Good luck finding your friends!" She splashed a potion of invisibility on Otto and then on herself.

Lily was devastated. "We have to find where they've taken our friends."

Mr. Anarchy said, "I think I have some ideas. I know that Otto and Emma had another base in the desert. They have a large prison in the stronghold."

"We have to go there." Lily felt helpless.

Michael agreed. "I heard them talk about their stronghold in the desert when I was trapped in the cold biome."

"Which desert? There are several desert biomes on this server." Lily's head began to spin.

Michael took out a map. "I guess we'll have to visit all of them."

"That's an impossible search—it will take forever." Lily paced, and her eyes welled with tears.

"We will find them," Mr. Anarchy said. "I think I know the way. Follow me."

Lily looked at Michael and shrugged. They followed Mr. Anarchy. But as the trio left the village, they spotted Matthew up ahead.

"Matthew! We have so much to tell you! Emma and Otto have trapped our friends on the server, but we don't know where." Lily spoke quickly.

"We think they are in the desert biome," added Michael.

Matthew said, "I know where they are."

"How?" Mr. Anarchy asked.

"They kidnapped me, right after you escaped," said Matthew, looking over their shoulders. "They held me their fortress in the desert biome."

"I didn't escape," Mr. Anarchy said. "I was captured by Otto and Emma, too. But it was weird—I was down by the ocean, collecting the gravel you said you needed for your experiments, and Otto and Emma TPed right to me. It's like they knew I'd be there."

"That is strange," Lily said. "Matthew, did they know exactly where you'd be?"

"Yeah, something like that," Matthew said, hurrying past them. He called over his shoulder, "Come on, let's get going."

Lily and Michael followed, but as the group left Lisimi Village in search of their trapped friends, night began to set in.

"We have to TP there," suggested Matthew.

"Do you think we should wait until it's morning?" Lily asked. "It might be too dangerous to travel at night."

"I don't think we should waste any time," Michael said. "We'll just have to deal with the hostile mobs."

"I guess you're right," Lily remarked. "Ilana gave me a potion of night vision. We should drink this so we can have an advantage during the trip."

As Lily handed out the potion, hostile mobs spawned in the dimly lit village. Zombies lumbered through the town. Lily sprinted toward an undead mob and attacked it with her diamond sword. Matthew and Michael battled a cluster of skeletons that shot arrows at the group.

Two Endermen walked past, and one of them spotted Mr. Anarchy and shrieked as it teleported toward him. He tried to escape by running to the shoreline, but it was too late. He wasn't fast enough, and he was destroyed by the lanky, block-carrying mob.

Lily, Matthew, and Michael were immersed in their own battles and couldn't help Mr. Anarchy. After a tough battle, Lily was relieved when she destroyed the last remaining zombie, but she didn't see the silent, green time bomb that was creeping up behind her.

Kaboom!

The creeper destroyed Lily. When she respawned in her bed, she reached for her sword and sprinted into the thick of the night in search of her friends. Lily reached the heart of Lisimi Village where the hostile mob battle had just taken place, but her friends' battle was over. She didn't see Michael, Matthew, or Mr. Anarchy.

Lily called out their names again and again, but there was no response.

She ran to Matthew's house, where Mr. Anarchy was also staying, but it was empty. She raced to Michael's house next, but it was empty, too. Lily was alone. She walked back to her house and climbed into bed. She'd wait out the night and find help and hope in the morning.

9
SECRETS

The sun shined as Lily jumped out of bed and raced toward the cottage window to peek outside. She put on her armor and left the cottage, spotting Matthew almost right away. "Where did you go last night? I was looking for you."

"Otto trapped Mr. Anarchy and Michael. He tried to trap me, but I escaped. Come with me, and we can try and save them," Matthew explained.

"To the desert?" questioned Lily.

"Yes," he replied.

The duo walked through the town and past Juan the Butcher, who held out a hand to stop them. "Are you leaving town?"

"We have to find our friends. They've been trapped in the desert by Otto and Emma," Lily told Juan.

"Be careful. Otto and Emma are very tricky players. And watch out for Mr. Anarchy. He said he is on your side, but I am not convinced. I was inside my home last night avoiding the mobs, but I could swear I heard voices that sounded like Mr. Anarchy's, Otto's, and Emma's. It sounded more like they were promising to help him get home than like they were taking him captive." Juan wished them well.

Lily and Matthew just looked at each other, eyebrows raised. "Thanks for telling us, Juan," Lily said. Then she turned to Matthew. "We had better go." He nodded, and the two left town.

After they'd been walking for a while, Lily asked Matthew, "Do you think Mr. Anarchy is on our side?"

Matthew was quiet for a long time. When he finally responded, he surprised Lily by saying, "If I tell you something, will you promise not to be mad?"

"What? Of course!"

Matthew fumbled with his words. "Well. Um. I'm—"

Roar!

Lily and Matthew looked up at the sound and saw the Ender Dragon spawn in the skies above them. They looked for shelter, but the open, grassy biome they walked through offered none.

"We can't battle that beast on our own!" Lily cried.

Matthew looked at Lily. "I—I have to go," he said, and he splashed a potion of invisibility on himself and disappeared.

"Matthew!" Lily screamed. She was left to battle the Ender Dragon on her own. Her heart was beating fast. She grabbed her diamond sword and struck the side of the dragon, but she was no match for this powerful, flying, hostile mob.

Lily was barely surviving the battle with the Ender Dragon, but then thunder boomed and rain fell on the ground, and skeletons and zombies started spawning in the distance. The dragon's large, scaly, gray wing slammed into Lily, and she lost a heart. At the same time, a skeleton shot an arrow that pierced her leg.

There was nobody there to help her or even hear her cries for help. Lily ran toward the dragon and tried to pound the beast with her diamond sword, but it was pointless. A sea of arrows flew in her direction, destroying her.

When Lily respawned in her bed, she was relieved to see Simon standing in her living room.

"How did you escape?" asked Lily.

"It wasn't easy." He hurried on. "There's no time. I have a lot to tell you."

Rain was still falling, and skeletons, zombies, and Endermen were spawning around Lisimi Village. A zombie ripped Lily's door off of its hinges.

Simon lunged at the zombie and clobbered the vacant-eyed mob with his diamond sword.

"We have to battle," Simon cried.

Simon and Lily sprinted to the center of the cluster of zombies. Simon splashed a potion on the zombies and Lily struck the undead mob with her sword, weakening it. When the last zombie was destroyed, Simon said, "We have to get out of here."

"We need to save our friends," Lily exclaimed.

"That's what I wanted to tell you. Some of them aren't our friends," Simon warned Lily.

"I think I've realized that!" Lily said. "Matthew abandoned me when I was battling an Ender Dragon on my own."

"What happened to the Ender Dragon?" asked Simon.

"I'm not sure, why?" asked Lily.

"Because I think I see it flying toward us!" Simon screamed.

10
ESCAPE PLANS

Lily gasped as the dragon flew toward them. "Not again!"

The two aimed their bows at the dragon, unleashing a sea of arrows. As they shielded themselves in the doorway, they watched the dragon explode. Without pausing for rest, Simon and Lily sprinted into the heart of the town, dodging skeletons' arrows and narrowly escaping zombie attacks.

"Watch out!" Lily warned Simon.

A powerful spider jockey spawned behind Simon. The skeleton shot an arrow at Simon's back.

Lily shot an arrow at the skeleton and then ran toward the bony beast riding the spider and splashed a potion on it, weakening both the skeleton and the spider. Simon attacked the spider with his diamond sword. Lily also grabbed her diamond sword and plunged it into the bony skeleton. It was destroyed, and while Simon annihilated the spider, Lily leaned down to pick up the bone it had dropped.

Lily looked up to see three zombies lumbering toward them. "Don't put your sword away," Lily said to Simon as she ran through the soggy village, ready to attack the undead beasts that terrorized the town.

Lily slammed her diamond sword into the zombie. She could see Juan the Butcher running toward her, and she called out, "Stay away!"

Juan didn't listen. As Lily and Simon battled the three zombies, they saw a new horde of zombies turn a corner and appear next to Juan. One of the zombies attacked Juan, and when zombie bit him Juan transformed into a ghastly, lumbering zombie villager.

"Do you have a golden apple and a potion?" Lily asked Simon. Simon clobbered two zombies and looked at his inventory. "Yes!"

"Then you have to save Juan!" Lily cried as she battled the remaining zombies.

Simon hurried over to Juan and helped him turn back into a regular villager.

"Thank you," Juan said gratefully.

Simon warned Juan to stay away. "Go back to your butcher shop. It's not safe for you here."

Lily sprinted to Simon's side and battled the zombies that trekked through their village, ripping doors off of hinges and terrorizing the villagers.

With their diamond swords and bottles of potion, they were able to destroy multiple zombies, but more zombies kept spawning.

"There has to be a spawner around here," Simon yelped as he slammed his sword into another vacant-eyed zombie.

"You're probably right, but I don't think this is the time to hunt for the zombie spawner." Lily barely spit out the words as she annihilated a horde of zombies that had cornered her against a wall by the village library.

"Watch out!"

Four creepers were silently lurking behind Simon. He dove out of the way, avoiding their powerful blast. As he escaped the creepers, he accidentally locked eyes with a lanky Enderman. The Endermen let out a high-pitched shriek and teleported to Simon.

"Run to the water! I'll come with you," Lily advised her friend. She spotted an army of skeletons and zombies marching into the heart of Lisimi Village. Lily knew they were about to face an intense battle, and she had a plan. When they reached the shore, she gave Simon a bottle of potion.

"What's this?" Simon asked.

"It's a potion of water breathing. We should drink this and hide under the sea for a while. It's too dangerous here." Lily gulped the potion and jumped into the deep blue water. Simon followed. The Enderman also jumped into the water, but the water destroyed the hostile mob.

They swam deep underneath the sea. "I hope we find an underwater temple," Simon said. "Maybe there's still time to look for some treasure."

Lily replied, "I hope so, too, but I don't see any guardians. And if we did find an ocean monument, it would probably be looted, since Matthew spent so much time exploring this biome."

Simon agreed. Matthew was always under the water, searching for treasures. Now that they suspected Matthew was evil, they both hoped he hadn't placed any booby traps in the ocean biome. He might even have a secret underwater headquarters in the ocean biome.

"Should we continue to explore the ocean biome?" questioned Lily. She knew that it was their only escape from the perpetually rainy Lisimi Village, but they had been swimming for a while and they hadn't spotted any underwater monuments. A guardian hadn't even attacked them.

Simon suggested, "Why don't we swim to the shore?"

Lily liked Simon's idea. She added, "I bet this potion is going to wear off soon, so that is a fantastic idea."

They swam to the ocean's surface. Simon called out, "Lily, look over there. Do you see land?"

Lily exclaimed, "I do! I see land!"

They swam toward the land. As they approached the shore, they saw large mushrooms sprouting from the ground.

"It's Mushroom Island!"

11
MOOSHROOMS

Simon and Lily climbed onto the shore of Mushroom Island. Lily was excited. This was a peaceful biome, and she knew they needed to take a break and figure out a plan to save all of their friends and stop their enemies. "Look, there's a mooshroom!" she cried. "Let's go milk it. I'd love some mushroom stew."

Simon tagged along behind Lily as she walked over to the mooshroom and milked the spotted animal, offering some stew to Simon.

"Thanks." He devoured the stew. Simon didn't realize how hungry he was until he started eating the savory stew.

Lily ate her portion of stew and put her bowl down.

"What's the matter?" asked Simon.

"Do you hear that?" Lily asked. "I hear someone talking."

Simon stood silently. "Yes, I do hear something."

Simon and Lily walked in the direction of the voices. Lily clutched her diamond sword, prepared for battle. She didn't want to assume that whoever was on Mushroom Island was bad, but after everything they'd been through she wanted to be cautious. The last thing she wanted was to be destroyed and forced to respawn in the middle of rainy Lisimi Village, where she would have to battle a never-ending group of zombies, skeletons, and Endermen again.

"I think I see something up ahead," Simon said, and he ran in front of Lily.

Lily spotted two people standing by a small house made out of a mushroom. As she walked toward them, Simon advised, "I think you should put the sword away. It might scare them."

Lily reluctantly placed her diamond sword back in her inventory. "I guess you're right. But if they attack us, we had better have a plan."

Simon and Lily didn't have time to come up with a plan, because the two girls spotted them and walked over.

"Hello." One of the girls spoke quickly; she appeared quite frazzled and nervous. "Are you the folks from the building competition?"

"No. What's that?" asked Simon.

The girl responded, "We were both invited to this server to participate in a building competition. Once we accepted the invitation, we were zapped into the game."

Simon and Lily looked at each other. That sounded like the work of many of their griefer enemies. "We're also trapped," Simon explained. "I'm Simon, and this is my friend Lily. We were trapped on the server a while ago."

Lily added, "I know how painful the first few days on the server are and how scary it is to live in the real Minecraft world."

"I'm Sarah," said one of the girls. "And this is my friend Georgia. I can't believe someone would zap us into the Overworld."

Georgia said, "It's been more than a few days. We've been on Mushroom Island for a while. You are the first people we've met."

Sarah explained, "We were too scared to leave the island. I tried to convince Georgia to build a boat and set sail, but she just wanted to stay on Mushroom Island."

"There are no hostile mobs on Mushroom Island, and I didn't want to have to battle any mobs. I couldn't imagine how terrifying it would be to encounter them in the real world when they're so scary in the game." Georgia shuddered at the thought of battling hostile mobs.

Lily shook her head. "It is awful. At the moment, our village is under constant attack from hostile mobs. We came here to escape."

"But we can't stick around this island. Our good friends are trapped in the desert." Simon told Georgia and Sarah about Mr. Anarchy and the other griefers, Otto and Emma.

"And don't forget about Matthew," Lily reminded him.

"Wow." Georgia was petrified. "This is an awful server. Not only are you trapped here, but you're being attacked by griefers."

"Yes," Simon agreed. "Would you like to help us find and free our friends in the desert? If you do, you can come back to our village and work with us. We are going to find a way to get back to the real world."

Sarah said, "I wish you luck finding your friends, but we don't want to get involved in any battles."

Georgia agreed. "I think Sarah and I will just figure out a way to get off of this server from Mushroom Island. If it was so easy to get zapped onto the server, it probably isn't that hard to get off."

"That's not true. It's harder than you think. We've been trying for a long time," Simon told them.

Sarah's eyes widened. "Really? How long?"

"I've lost track of time," Simon confessed.

"We did have good friends who escaped from the server." Lily didn't want Georgia and Sarah to lose hope, so she told them the story of the Prismarines.

Georgia asked if she could talk to Sarah in private, and Lily and Simon nodded. After the two new players spoke in a hushed whisper by a large mushroom, they walked back to Simon and Lily.

Sarah said, "We do want your help. We don't like being trapped on Mushroom Island. But we're scared."

"It's normal to be scared," Lily reassured them. "But you can't stay here and do nothing. We know who might have trapped you on this server, and if we don't defeat those griefers, there won't be any peace and none of us will escape."

"And they will keep zapping new people onto the server," Simon added. "I know how it feels to be zapped onto a server, and I don't want anyone else to have that awful experience. I know why I'm in this battle and how important it is to defeat the griefers."

Sarah sighed and asked, "What do you need us to do?"

Lily paced. "We have to come up with a plan. We know that our friends are trapped in the desert, and we have to travel there to free them."

Simon said, "Once we free them, we will battle the griefers. But this plan isn't as easy as it sounds."

Georgia was stunned. "It doesn't sound easy at all."

Sarah agreed. "This sounds like it's quite dangerous."

"It's worth it," said Lily.

"It's our only way out of here." Simon wished there was an easier way out. He wished he could use a cheat like he had many times while playing other video games. But there was no easy battle. This was similar to the moment in class when his teacher, Mrs. Sanders, had spotted him tossing a note. He had had to admit that he was the one who threw it or the entire class would have gotten in trouble. Sometimes, he knew, you just couldn't take the easy way out.

Sarah was having second thoughts. "Maybe we will stay here after all."

Georgia looked at her friend. "That sounds like a good idea."

Sarah asked, "Can you come back for us when you're done rescuing your friends and battling the awful griefers who trapped us on this server?"

Lily couldn't believe they were backing out of the plan. She wanted to lecture them on the importance of working together, but there was no time to talk.

Sarah shrieked, "Zombies!"

Lily gasped as an army of zombies marched through the peaceful mushroom biome, ready to attack.

12
ZOMBIE ATTACK

"The griefers know we're here," Lily called out as she ran toward the undead beasts.

"The zombies are so much scarier in real life." Georgia's voice shook.

"Zombies aren't too hard to battle. Just use your diamond sword," Lily called over her shoulder.

Simon nodded and reached for his inventory. "Lily and I have a bunch of potions. We'll splash them on the zombies to weaken them."

Georgia stood frozen. Her hands were shaking almost too hard for her to hold her diamond sword. She watched as Simon and Lily splashed potions on the zombies and then struck the beasts with their diamond swords. Taking a deep breath, Sarah ran into the fray to fight alongside Simon and Lily. Georgia wanted to help, but she was too scared, and her new friends were too immersed in the battle to notice Georgia.

"Good job!" Simon called out to Sarah as she struck two zombies and destroyed them.

Sarah picked up the rotten flesh the zombies dropped, then turned around to look for Georgia. "Come on!" she called. "It's not as hard you think!" Lily splashed more potions on the zombies that lumbered toward the group. "We have to find the monster spawner. Otto, Emma, and whoever they're working with must have placed one on this island."

Sarah obliterated three of the weakened zombies. She was growing more confident. She called to her friend again. "Georgia. We need your help. If you aren't going to battle the zombies, can you search for the monster spawner?"

Georgia couldn't imagine going off on her own. What if the griefer who had placed the spawner was standing beside it waiting for her? She had no other choice; she had to join the others in battle. With a shudder, she lunged at a zombie. Her sword plunged into the beast, destroying it. "I did it!" she called out, but the others were too busy destroying their own monsters to notice Georgia.

There were only a couple of zombies left, and the group was relieved. "Maybe there isn't a spawner," Lily said while clobbering the remaining zombies.

"You're right. The griefers could have just summoned the undead horde without placing a spawner," said Simon.

"In any case," Lily said, looking around the quiet island, "I think we should head to the desert biome as soon as possible. We aren't getting anywhere sticking around this island."

"Before we go, we need to get our energy back," Simon told them.

"Let's drink some mushroom stew," Lily said as she walked toward a spotted mooshroom.

The gang gathered around her while she milked the peaceful animal. They all ate the stew and drank milk. When their energy and health bars were full, they walked to the shoreline.

Georgia suggested, "If we're going to leave the island, I can build us some boats."

"Georgia makes some of the best boats in the Overworld," Sarah agreed.

"I can craft something very quickly." Georgia took out wooden planks from her inventory and started to construct a boat. "It's more important to have a functional boat than a fancy one right now. I don't want to be here if more zombies spawn."

Simon and Lily were impressed with Georgia's building skills. Within minutes, she had built four small wooden boats. They each hopped in a boat and set sail for the desert. As the boats floated next to each other, Simon checked his map. "Just follow me," he said, turning his boat once he got his bearings. "According to the map, we don't have to travel very far until we reach the desert. Since we're leaving Mushroom Island anyway, we should try to find where are friends are being held."

Georgia and Sarah were beginning to feel comfortable in this new world. "I think Georgia and I are ready to help you face those griefers," Sarah said, looking to her friend for confirmation.

Georgia nodded. "I know I was scared of battling the zombies, but once I started to battle them, I realized it wasn't as scary as I imagined," she confessed.

Simon nodded. "Sometimes thinking about something we're afraid of is actually scarier than doing it."

As the sky turned dark and rain fell on the sea, the peaceful journey on the water grew perilous.

"What's happening?" Georgia asked.

"Are the griefers following us?" Lily looked for other boats that might be traveling near them, but she didn't see anything.

"They must have summoned a storm," Simon said, looking up at the sky.

Thunder boomed, and a lightning bolt hit the water.

"Oh no!" cried Sarah.

The next lightning bolt struck Georgia's boat.

"Georgia!" Sarah cried.

There was no reply. Georgia had vanished.

13
DESERT BATTLE

The rain stopped and Simon called out, "I see land!"

"Where did Georgia go?" Tears filled Sarah's eyes. She didn't care about reaching land; she just wanted to find Georgia.

"She probably got zapped back to the real world. That happens when people are struck by lightning," Simon replied.

"Then I want to be struck by lightning, too!" Sarah sniffled.

Lily sighed. "I wish it was that easy. We've tried. Georgia was just incredibly lucky."

"We'll find our way back home. Don't worry," Simon reassured Sarah as they docked their boats on the shore.

Sarah nodded sadly, and she and Lily followed Simon as he placed his boat against a dock and hopped onto the beach.

"Are you going to be okay, Sarah?" Lily asked.

Sarah nodded. "I'm going to miss Georgia, though."

Lily patted Sarah comfortingly on the back. "Of course. But I still have hope that we'll find a way to get off the server, and you'll be able to see Georgia again then."

Sarah squared her shoulders and nodded again, more firmly this time. "Okay," she said. "So, which way do we go?"

Simon studied the map. "We just have to travel through this grassy biome, and then we'll reach the desert."

Sarah paused, squinting at the horizon. "I think I see the desert in the distance."

"You're right!" Lily was excited, but she was also secretly nervous about battling the powerful griefers. She couldn't stop thinking about how they hadn't taken any damage, no matter how powerful her attacks had been.

"Let's pick up the pace a little," Simon called to them.

The three friends ran as fast at they could through the grassy biome toward the sandy desert.

When they reached the flat desert biome, dotted with cacti, Simon looked around. "I don't see a desert temple."

"We know it's here. We'll find it," Lily said hopefully.

"Ouch!" Sarah grabbed her arm. "I was just struck by an arrow."

Lily scanned the area for signs of a griefer. It was too light for skeletons to be spawning. "I don't see anybody."

Suddenly, a barrage of arrows flew through the desert sky. Lily dodged a couple, but several more pierced her skin, and she lost a few hearts.

"I see them!" Simon called out.

"Where?" Lily grabbed her sword.

"By the sand dune!" Simon sprinted toward the griefers.

Lily spotted Matthew standing in front of the griefer army. She screamed, "You! You left me alone with the Ender Dragon, and now you're attacking us? I thought you were our friend."

Matthew barked orders at his soldiers. "Put your bows down. I need to talk to these people." He held his diamond sword at the ready and walked over to Sarah. "Who are you?"

Sarah flinched and stammered, "S-Sarah."

"So you made it," Matthew said.

"What's that supposed to mean?" Lily demanded.

"Never mind," Matthew said. "It doesn't matter. I'm here to capture all of you and place you in the prison with your friends."

"You can't capture us," Lily hollered.

"You're outnumbered," Matthew said, pointing to his large army of griefers, "and you can't go back home because Mr. Anarchy has summoned a never-ending storm over Lisimi Village. I'm sure your villager friends Juan, Fred, and Emily have been turned into zombie villagers by now. You'll have nobody to help you when you go back there. So you have no choice but to be my prisoner."

Simon leapt at Matthew, and his diamond sword ripped into Matthew's arm. "Never! We will never be your prisoner."

"And we don't believe Mr. Anarchy is doing that," Lily added. "He's changed—unlike you."

"Are you sure about that?" Michael asked. "What if Otto and Emma promised him a real way home instead of just more of your failed attempts? That's how they convinced me to join them and to help them kidnap Mr. Anarchy the first time. It was only a matter of time before they convinced him, too." Matthew picked a potion of harming from his inventory and splashed it on Simon, leaving him with only two hearts. "Mr. Anarchy and I finally have what you could never give us: hope that we'll be able to go home. We just have to prove to Otto and Emma that we're worthy—by destroying your village."

Lily's head was spinning as she considered everything Matthew was saying. What if he was telling the truth? If they were destroyed, would they respawn in a village full of zombies? As Matthew raised his sword again, moving closer to Simon, she was suddenly terrified for her friend, and she cried out, "Stop!"

"Are you ready to surrender?" Matthew asked.

"Yes," she replied.

"No, we're not," Simon said angrily.

Sarah agreed with Lily. "We have no other choice, Simon."

Simon was exhausted. He had lost too many hearts and he needed to restore his energy. He looked down, sighing, and uttered the words, "We surrender."

"I couldn't hear you." Matthew smirked. "What did you say?"

"You heard me," Simon said, annoyance creeping into his voice.

"You're my prisoners," Matthew announced, and he ordered the griefers to escort them to the desert temple.

Lily, Simon, and Sarah followed Matthew in silence. Lily didn't like being helpless and was losing hope as they reached the temple. But her energy lifted when they neared the temple's entrance and saw Michael, Peter, Robin, Warren, and Ilana. Her friends were locked in battle with Mr. Anarchy.

Matthew charged into the heart of the battle, hollering, "What's going on here?"

"Help!" Mr. Anarchy could barely speak.

"Where are Otto and Emma?" Matthew demanded.

Lily handed Simon a potion of strength, and he quickly gulped the powerful brew down and rushed at Matthew. Simon slammed his diamond sword into Matthew's back.

"Hey!" Matthew turned around.

Lily and Sarah also struck Matthew, and he lost another two hearts.

"Help!" Matthew called out to the griefer soldiers who stood by and watched.

"No," one of the griefer soldiers called back. "This is your battle."

Lily looked at the griefer solider. "Help us!" she cried.

"Gladly," another griefer solider replied.

"No!" Matthew screamed.

Matthew only had one heart left, and his army had betrayed him. But Lily called off the attack. "We don't want to destroy him," she said. "We have no idea where he'll respawn." She looked at Matthew. "Isn't this ironic? Now you're our prisoner."

"No, he's not!" a voice cried out. Everyone whirled around to see Otto standing with Emma on a portal to the Nether. "Mr. Anarchy! Matthew! Come here!"

Lily, Simon and Sarah shot arrows at Matthew and Mr. Anarchy, but they dodged them, using their last bit of energy to sprint to the portal. The griefers ignited it and disappeared into a sea of purple mist.

14
NEVER SAY NETHER

"We can't let them escape!" Michael called out.
"Let's build a Nether portal," suggested Peter.

Lily crafted a portal to the Nether and the gang hopped aboard. After she ignited the portal and purple mist rose around the group, Lily introduced them to Sarah. Sarah nodded a nervous hello just as they arrived in the hostile world.

Sarah shook as she stepped off the portal, and Lily looked over at her. "I think the Nether was trickiest place to acclimate to, and it's a lot more challenging than the Overworld. But stick with me, and I'll help you through it."

"Thanks," Sarah replied, and she walked next to Lily.

Simon was pleased to be reunited with his old friends. He moved to walk next to Michael and asked,

"Do you have any idea where the griefers might be hiding?"

"No," Michael said. "We were trapped in that prison until right before you showed up, when we staged an uprising. I didn't manage to overhear any of their plans."

Ilana added, "I don't think they had a plan for the Nether. I think they just needed a quick escape. I'm sure we'll find them."

"I can't believe Matthew is a griefer," Lily said. She still couldn't believe that he had abandoned her to fight the Ender Dragon alone.

"I know! And Mr. Anarchy, too," Simon added. "I really thought his change of heart was for real this time."

"Watch out!" Ilana warned. "Ghasts!"

A group of ghasts flew through the Nether sky, spitting fireballs in their direction.

Sarah was the first to battle the fiery mob, using her fist to punch the ghasts' fireballs back at them, destroying two immediately.

They dropped rare ghast tears. Ilana noticed and hurried to pick them up. "These are very useful for brewing the potion for regeneration," she clarified. "I'm an alchemist."

"That's good to know," Sarah said with a smile.

Michael threw a snowball at a blaze and hit it. "Bulls-eye!" he called out.

"You guys, I see the griefers!" Simon called, distracting them from their battle. He pointed toward a far-off Nether fortress, where four distant figures were running for shelter.

Though too busy to turn and see the griefers disappearing into the fortress, the gang hurried to finish their fight. When the final ghast and blaze were destroyed, they ran to the majestic Nether fortress. "We know you're in here!" Simon called. "There's no escape."

There was no response.

"Are you sure they went in here?" asked Ilana.

"Yes," Simon said, annoyed. "I saw them run inside."

The gang carefully inspected the rooms. Sarah let out a cry of surprise when she almost walked into the lava room.

Lily heard Sarah's cry from the room next door, and was about to check on her when she heard Simon screaming for help. She turned and sprinted toward the sounds of his cries.

"Help!" Simon wailed. As he came into view, Lily saw Mr. Anarchy pointing a diamond sword at Simon's chest.

"Where are the others?" Lily questioned, aiming her bow at Mr. Anarchy.

"We have them!" Michael called out, walking out of the darkness down the hall.

Lily released her arrow, and as Mr. Anarchy shielded himself, Simon made his escape and raced to Lily. Lily leapt at Mr. Anarchy and struck him with her diamond sword. He was down to one heart.

Simon and Lily cornered Mr. Anarchy. Lily shouted, "You're our prisoner now."

From close to the fortress's entrance, Peter called out, "We have Otto and Emma."

"And I have Matthew," Sarah said, having snuck up behind Lily and aimed her bow and arrow at the griefer.

Lily, Simon, and Sarah walked Mr. Anarchy and Matthew over to the other griefers.

"You have to stop causing problems in the Overworld and zapping new people like Sarah onto the server," Lily said.

"Don't blame me," Mr. Anarchy said. "I haven't trapped any new players on the server since you captured me."

"I don't believe you," Sarah said. She was getting more confident after several successful battles. "Who zapped me onto this server? Who lied to me and said I was going to be part of a building competition?"

Nobody replied.

"It doesn't matter," Warren said. "All four of these griefers are done."

"I hope you'll enjoy living in a never-ending storm," Simon said. "Since you started the storm in Lisimi Village, and that's where we're taking you to be held captive."

The gang was ready to craft a portal and take the criminals to their village when three blazes flew into the Nether fortress. One of them shot a fireball at the group, and it struck Mr. Anarchy, destroying him. "Mr. Anarchy!" Lily cried out.

Simon struck a blaze with a snowball and destroyed it. Sarah obliterated the final blaze with an arrow.

"We have to go back to the Overworld now," Michael ordered them. "We have to find Mr. Anarchy."

15
THE SEARCH FOR MR. ANARCHY

"We can't take the other griefers with us while we search for Mr. Anarchy," Simon said. "Lily, Sarah, and I will hunt for Mr. Anarchy. You guys should escort Matthew, Otto, and Emma back to Lisimi Village. We'll come back as soon as we can to help battle the mobs created by the storm."

Michael said, "I know the desert. I think I should go with you guys."

Ilana nodded. "That's a good plan. Don't worry about us—we'll take care of these sinister griefers."

They crafted a portal and everyone hopped aboard. Lily held a sword against Matthew's chest as they made their way back to the Overworld. They emerged in the heart of Lisimi Village. It was still raining.

Juan the Butcher raced over to them.

Lily asked, "Where are Emily and Fred? Were they turned into zombie villagers?"

"No. They are hiding in my shop," replied Juan.

Lily was relieved and was happy to be back in Lisimi Village, but she couldn't stay, even just to visit her bungalow. She wished everyone well and left with Sarah, Michael, and Simon on their journey to the sandy biome.

Michael looked back as they exited Lisimi Village. He watched Ilana, Peter, and Warren march Matthew, Otto, and Emma off to the town's bedrock prison. Michael remarked, "I'm glad they'll be in prison and now we won't have to deal with their antics. If we can just get the storm over Lisimi Village to stop, we can focus on making our way back home."

Lily added, "Maybe we'll finally be able to finish our treasure hunt with Peter."

Michael smiled. "That seems like a good idea."

"If we want to get to the desert faster, I saw some rails we could use," Lily said. She also knew a spot where they could find minecarts.

Once they were in the minecarts, they sped to the desert. Lily jumped out of the cart and walked into the desert temple. "I don't see Mr. Anarchy."

Michael led them to a room at the back of the temple. "This is where he was staying, so this should be where he respawned. I guess he left the desert right away."

Just then, they heard a footstep in the hallway behind them.

"Who's there?" Simon called.

A man wearing jeans and a blue shirt walked down the hall. "I was one of the soldiers who guarded this temple," he said. "But everybody has left."

"Where did they go?" questioned Lily.

"Once you followed our leaders to the Nether, everyone left the desert. Nobody wanted to be here."

Sarah asked, "Did you see Mr. Anarchy respawn here?"

"Yes," he admitted. "He also changed skins. When I knew him, he wore an all-blue suit. Once he respawned, he changed his skin to black pants and a green shirt."

Lily was about to ask the soldier another question when an arrow pierced her arm.

"Mr. Anarchy!" Sarah cried.

Lily spun around to face her attacker. Mr. Anarchy was dressed in the skin that the soldier had described. He shot another arrow. Lily sprinted toward him and splashed a potion of harming on him. Her friends joined her, and almost immediately, they had surrounded and subdued their enemy.

"Stop!" Mr. Anarchy cried out.

"We are taking you back to Lisimi Village," Michael hollered.

"Never!" he screamed and splashed a potion of invisibility on himself.

"Where did he go?" Lily said, dismayed.

The soldier said, "He can't have gone very far. I know that he is running low on resources, and without our army, he has no help."

"We have to find him now," Simon said. He wanted to see Mr. Anarchy in the bedrock prison in Lisimi Village once again.

The soldier added, "He really wants to get back to the real world. At first, when Otto and Emma kidnapped him, he resisted. But when even Matthew told him that they could send him home, he started doing whatever they asked. He must still be hoping they'll help him."

Sarah searched the area around the desert temple. She knew the sooner they captured Mr. Anarchy, the closer she would be to getting home. Sarah called out, "I think I see him!" and charged at the master griefer.

"I see him, too!" Simon replied, and he followed Sarah toward Mr. Anarchy.

But Sarah had already made the capture. She was standing next to Mr. Anarchy with her diamond sword pointed toward his chest. "Game over, Mr. Anarchy," she said triumphantly.

16
IT CAN'T BE THE END

"I wouldn't say the game is over," Mr. Anarchy said, looking at the group of friends who had him surrounded. "I'd say it has paused."

"We're going to make sure you don't go back to your old tricks," Simon said, holding his sword against Mr. Anarchy's back.

Mr. Anarchy was cornered. There was no escape.

Mr. Anarchy stared at the lone soldier, hoping he would help him escape, but the soldier approached them and offered no help. "I'd never help you," he said.

"Are you going to stay here by yourself?" Lily asked the lone soldier. "Would you like to come back to Lisimi Village with us?"

"I just want to focus on trying to get back home. I don't want to settle into a village," the soldier replied.

"We are working on getting home, too," Lily told the soldier.

"Really?"

"Yes. Come with us," added Simon.

"Okay," the soldier said. "I'm George, and I'd love to come back with you guys and work on ways to get back home."

With George's help, the friends escorted Mr. Anarchy to the minecarts and traveled back to Lisimi Village.

Though rain still poured down on the village and the townspeople were still battling mobs, the friends were met by cheers when they returned with Mr. Anarchy. They hurried to the bedrock prison and opened the door, then marched Mr. Anarchy inside.

"This will be a good place for you to think about all the hurt you've caused, Mr. Anarchy," Lily said. "Even if you only griefed because you hoped Otto and Emma would send you home, it still wasn't okay."

"I'd do it again if it meant I could go home," Mr. Anarchy said. "I'm not sorry."

"We will get back home," Lily told Mr. Anarchy. "And we'll do it without hurting anyone else. Maybe we'll even help you get off this server, too."

Mr. Anarchy looked up in surprise. "Why would you help me?"

"Because everyone deserves to leave this server and get back home," Lily said. "I'm sure you have people back home who miss you, too."

Mr. Anarchy ducked his head, but Lily was almost certain she heard a sniffle.

"That goes for the rest of you, too," she said, starting to shut the cell door.

"Wait!" Matthew cried.

"What do you want?" Simon asked, tensing.

"I—" Matthew hunched his shoulders and looked at the floor. "I want to apologize. I'm the one who trapped Sarah on this server."

Sarah gasped. "How could you?"

"I wanted to go home so badly. I told myself that anybody in my position would do the same thing if it gave them a chance to save themselves." He looked around at the group. "But I can see that I was wrong. None of you would betray the others. I respect that."

Lily nodded. "Well, maybe with some time in prison, you can learn from it, too."

Matthew nodded. "I think I will. But before you lock me in, there's one more thing I'd like to do. I know how to stop the storm—I'm the one who started it."

17
ORIGINAL PLANS

Everyone cheered as the rain stopped and the sun came out over Lisimi Village. With a small smile, Lily nodded to Matthew, and then they shut the door to the bedrock cell, trapping their tormentors.

Peter walked over to Lily, Simon, Michael, and Sarah. "Can we still finish our treasure hunt?"

"Yes," Lily said with a smile. "We all need some treasure to replenish our inventories."

"George and I would like to join you, too," Sarah announced.

"Of course," Lily said. "The more the merrier."

As the group walked out of town, Sarah pulled some cake from her inventory and offered it around. "I was saving this for a special day," she said.

"I really feel like we're about to start a new beginning," Warren said. "After this treasure hunt, we can concentrate on getting back to the real world."

Finally, they came to the temple Peter had asked them to help him loot days before. Peter led the way deep into the cave and toward the stronghold and the dungeon where he had once found treasure.

"Watch out!" Lily warned as four creepers silently lurked in the stronghold. The gang used their arrows to destroy the mobs. The creepers exploded and the gang shielded themselves.

As they walked down the stairs toward the dungeon, an arrow hit Lily's thigh. She called out to the others. "Skeletons!"

The dimly lit stronghold was a breeding ground for hostile mobs, but the friends were prepared to battle whatever mobs they encountered. Lily shot an arrow at the skeleton, causing it to lose hearts.

The skeleton aimed and struck Lily with another arrow. She tried to dodge the arrows from the skeleton but couldn't.

Just as she was losing hearts, George leapt at the skeleton attacking Lily and struck the bony beast with his diamond sword. Sarah and Robin joined George and also pounded their diamond swords into the skeleton. Working together, they destroyed the skeleton, and the others like it.

Peter led them to the dungeon and everyone marveled at the numerous unopened treasure chests in the room. Peter sighed. "I am so relieved. I was worried that somebody would unearth the treasure before we had a chance to make it to the dungeon."

Lily suggested, "Peter, why don't you open the first chest?"

Peter opened the treasure chest. A fetid odor tainted the air of the musty dungeon.

"Yuck!" Peter was disappointed. "It's just a chest filled with rotten flesh."

Lily tried to make him feel better. "We can still use rotten flesh, even if we can't eat it."

"Open another one," Lily told Peter.

Peter paused before he opened the next treasure chest. He was afraid all of the chests would be filled with rotten flesh. When he finally gathered enough nerve to open the second chest, he wailed, "More rotten flesh!"

"This is awful," said Michael.

"I don't think they're all filled with rotten flesh. There has to be some treasure in here," Lily said, and then she looked at Peter. "Open another one."

"No," Peter said. "I think I'm done."

"Just one more," Lily said.

Peter opened a third chest and smiled. "Diamonds! This one has diamonds!"

The group cheered and Peter distributed diamonds to everyone.

"Open the next one," Peter told Lily.

Lily opened up the chest. "Enchantment books!"

Lily watched as her friends opened up the remaining chests. There were no more chests filled with rotten flesh. They were filled with iron, gold ingots, and other treasures. The gang left the dungeon with inventories overflowing with treasure.

18
TREASURE

"We have treasure," Lily announced when they arrived in Lisimi Village.

"This calls for a celebration," Robin announced.

Emily, Juan, and Fred ran over to the group, and Peter told them about the treasure chests filled with rotten flesh and how happy they were to find chests filled with diamonds.

"We are about to have a feast to celebrate a successful treasure hunt. Would you like to join us?" Warren asked them.

All the townspeople and the villagers cheered and prepared for a feast.

They gathered in the center of the town and dined on cakes, meats, and the remaining mushroom stew that Lily had stored in her inventory.

Everyone sat around exchanging stories. Robin told tales of her time as a prisoner in the desert. Simon told the townspeople about how they followed and fought Matthew, Otto, Emma, and Mr. Anarchy in the Nether. George spoke about being a soldier who was forced to fight for Mr. Anarchy. "I'm so glad that I can be in this village now," George said at the end of his tale.

The townspeople were a captive audience, hardly able to believe how many battles the gang had fought in order to keep the village and everyone in it safe.

Lily listened eagerly to all of her friends' stories as well. She loved hearing about everyone else's adventures. When it was her turn to talk, she told everyone about meeting Sarah and how happy she was to have a new friend. As Lily ate a piece of cake, she realized how much she enjoyed small moments like these. There were always battles to fight, and one day she wanted to see her home again. But for now, she simply wanted to enjoy the cake and think about all the treasure in her inventory and the friends surrounding her. That was enough.

1
NEW ARRIVALS

Simon kept a close eye on his inventory. "We have to make sure there is enough wood."

"We'll be fine. If we run out of supplies, we'll just stop and get more." Michael dismissed Simon's comment.

"I don't like to start a project I can't finish." Simon was annoyed.

"We can finish it, but we might have to pause in the middle to get some more wood," Michael clarified.

Lily walked over. "What are you building?"

"We're building a carousel. I was thinking we could use some redstone," said Simon.

"That sounds like fun," replied Lily as she eyed their large roller coaster. She had built that coaster with Michael and Simon, and now they were building a carousel on their own. "You're building it right by the roller coaster?"

"Yes," explained Michael. "We want to make an amusement park."

Lily felt a lump in her throat. "It seems like a rather large project for two people."

"Do you think we need help?" asked Simon.

Lily tried to hide her disappointment. "I guess you can do it on your own."

"Is everything okay, Lily?" Michael put down his supplies and walked over to his friend.

"Yes." Lily wiped the tears from her eyes.

Simon rushed over. "What is it?"

"I feel left out. We always built everything together, and now you're doing this on your own. Why didn't you think to invite me?" She frowned.

"We just forgot. We didn't mean to upset you," Simon stammered.

"You forgot about me?" Lily was hurt.

"We always like building with you," Michael explained.

"Yes," Simon added. "We just walked over here and had the idea to build a carousel. Of course we were going to ask you."

Matthew thought for a moment. "I guess we've all gotten used to being a bit more independent since being trapped on the server. But we have to remember how important our friendships are, and work together as a team. Lily, would you please help us build this carousel?"

Lily smiled. "Thanks. I'd love to help you guys."

"Do you have any redstone?" Simon asked as he perused his inventory for the second time.

Lily studied her inventory and suggested, "An amusement park is a big project. Why don't we invite other people from the town to help? I'm sure Warren, Robin, Ilana, Peter, George, and Sarah would want to build an amusement park with us. And I bet there would be even more people excited about it, too."

"Yes, we should make this a team effort," Simon agreed.

"That's a fantastic idea," Michael exclaimed.

"Come with me," Lily said. "Let's ask the townspeople to help us." Her two friends followed her back toward Lisimi Village.

"I hope we find someone to help quickly. I really want to get back to work," Michael remarked.

As they walked, Lily thought about a name for the amusement park. "Should we name it Lisimi Land?"

"Or we can name it Adventure Park and make a bunch of adventure courses," suggested Simon.

"What about Fun Park?" Michael added.

As the trio bounced around various names for their amusement park, they stumbled upon two people who looked lost. The strangers stood by a tree, looking off in the direction of the town.

"Can you help us?" the girl, who was wearing a pink beret, called out. She was shaking and seemed very upset. "We see there is a town in the distance."

"I see an iron golem," said the boy, who was wearing a black suit.

"We're lost," admitted the girl.

"Are you okay?" Lily asked.

The girl in the pink beret shook as she spoke. "No. I think something has gone very wrong."

"Yes, incredibly wrong," added her friend. His voice cracked. "I think we are actually *in* a Minecraft game. We were playing, and we got zapped into this game."

Lily's heart started to beat rapidly. She couldn't believe more people had been zapped onto the server when all of the griefers responsible for sucking people into the game had been imprisoned. Seeing these two new people not only shocked her, it also scared her; she wondered who had zapped them on the server.

"Can you tell us your story?" Michael asked. "How were you zapped onto the server?"

Lily nodded encouragingly. "I know you're upset, but please, tell us what you can remember. We want to help you and this is an important step in figuring out how you were trapped on the server."

The girl wearing the pink beret introduced herself first. "I'm Blossom. I was playing on a server with my friends and then it just shut off."

"It's not that simple," the boy in the black suit added. "We were in the middle of unearthing treasure. It was so annoying because we lost the treasure, and now we're actually in Minecraft. I didn't even know that was possible."

Blossom explained how they were both playing Minecraft at her house when it happened. "The game shut off as we were unearthing the treasure, and when we turned our computers back on, the lights shut off in my house and we were zapped onto the server."

"That's awful," Lily exclaimed. "We know how hard it is to adjust, but we'll help you," she reassured them.

"But we have to find out who zapped them onto this server," Michael added.

"Yes, we do." Lily wondered if there was another griefer in the Overworld who had the power to zap people onto the server. Lily was terrified that there was an unknown, powerful griefer in the Overworld.

Michael uttered, "This isn't going to be easy."

Lily gave him a dirty look. She didn't want to frighten the newcomers.

Simon looked up at the sky. "It's almost night, and we have to get back to the village."

"Do you have a place where we can stay?" asked Blossom. "I can't bear to battle any hostile mobs in real life."

"Yes." Michael offered them a room in his house.

"Thanks," said the man in the black suit, and then he finally introduced himself. "I'm Sunny. I forgot to mention that when we were unearthing the treasure, we saw other treasure hunters, and they started to attack us."

"Do you think they had something to do with trapping you on the server?" asked Michael.

"I'm not sure," replied Sunny.

"What did they look like?" asked Simon.

"I didn't see them for very long, but they were wearing blue hats, which I thought was very strange," said Sunny.

"Blue hats. I don't know anyone who wears a blue hat." Lily tried to figure out who wanted Blossom and Sunny's treasure.

"Did you hear them call out any names?" questioned Michael.

Blossom stammered, "Um, no. It all happened so quickly. I wasn't paying attention; I just wanted to get the treasure and TP back to our village. And then the lights went out and we were trapped on this server."

"This is so similar to how we were trapped. Our parents were calling to us to stop playing because there was a powerful storm in our town, but we were trying to stop a gang of griefers from attacking our roller coaster. If only we had shut the computer down and stopped playing, we wouldn't be trapped on this server, too." Simon's eyes filled with tears.

"I'm sorry. I didn't mean to upset you." Blossom looked at Simon.

Lily didn't want to focus on the negative or the reason they were trapped on the server. She wanted to get to the bottom of this mystery. "We will find out who trapped you on this server," she declared.

"And you'll definitely get us home?" asked Blossom.

Lily opened her mouth to answer, but she didn't know how to respond.

Check out the rest of the
Unofficial Minetrapped Adventure series
and read what happens to Simon, Lily, and Michael:

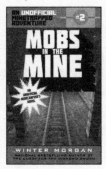

Trapped in the
Overworld
WINTER MORGAN

Mobs in the
Mine
WINTER MORGAN

Terror on a
Treasure Hunt
WINTER MORGAN

Ghastly Battle
WINTER MORGAN

Creeper Invasion
WINTER MORGAN

Attack of the
Ender Dragon
WINTER MORGAN

Available wherever books are sold!

DO YOU LIKE FICTION FOR MINECRAFTERS?

Read the
Unofficial Minecrafters Academy series!

Zombie Invasion
WINTER MORGAN

Skeleton Battle
WINTER MORGAN

Battle in the
Overworld
WINTER MORGAN

DO YOU LIKE FICTION FOR MINECRAFTERS?

Check out other unofficial Minecrafter adventures from Sky Pony Press!

Invasion of the Overworld

MARK CHEVERTON

Battle for the Nether

MARK CHEVERTON

Confronting the Dragon

MARK CHEVERTON

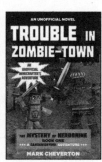

Trouble in Zombie-town

MARK CHEVERTON

The Quest for the Diamond Sword

WINTER MORGAN

The Mystery of the Griefer's Mark

WINTER MORGAN

The Endermen Invasion

WINTER MORGAN

Treasure Hunters in Trouble

WINTER MORGAN

Available wherever books are sold!